IN THE TIME OF THE "DENTED-PAN"

AND THE STRANGE QUIET

MASHUGA MOOSE WALKED DOWN TO THE MOOSE MERCANTILE, WHICH WAS NEXT TO THE "MASHUGA MOOSE CAFE." BEING A READING CHALLENGED MOOSE, HE DID THE BEST HE COULD TO READ THE MESSAGES WRITTEN ON THE STORE'S GLASS WINDOW.

THE BIGGEST LETTERS SEEMED TO SAY THAT THE STORE WAS CLOSED BECAUSE OF A PAN-DEMIC. THE YOUNG MOOSE, ALSO BEING A BIT DYSLEXIC DECIDED IN HIS BRAIN THAT THE WORDS THAT MEANT PAN-DEMIC SHOULD GO TOGETHER LIKE THIS, DENTED PAN.

ALLAN ROSEN-DUCAT

THIS BOOK IS DEDICATED TO THE
LOVING MEMORY OF MY BROTHER
LAWRENCE ADAM DUCAT,
AKA, "POPSY"

IN THE MIDST OF THE "DENTED-PAN
& THE STRANGE QUIET" MY BROTHER PASSED AWAY
FROM TYPE ONE DIABETES.
TO MY BROTHER, LARRY DUCAT,
HE SAW THE WORLD WITH LOVE FOR ALL PEOPLE GREAT AND SMALL.

THE DEEPEST OF GRATITUDE AND LOVE TO MY WIFE LIZ AND
FAMILY FOR RESPONDING TO MY CREATIVE PHANTASM
WITH HUMOR, LOVE AND SUPPORT.

CONTENTS

INTRODUCTION

"COVID-19" became a global health topic in November of 2019 when China announced the outbreak of the strain. In the spring of 2020, as "COVID-19" was spreading globally, countries around the globe closed all non-essential businesses as humans began at-home "social distancing."

The next day people around the world didn't go to work in an office or factory; the whole world became quiet. Wildlife living near these newly quieted places became confused. After all, humans were usually very, very noisy.

By day two of the "Quiet," all but gone were the sounds that wildlife had used to warn one another of the presence of humans. There weren't any planes in the sky or train horns to be heard. Most cars were left parked in their owners' driveways; they weren't needed for the family's daily commute to school and work. Wild animals that had been avoiding human noise every waking minute of their lives, now, cautiously visited these new quiet spaces. They knew something had changed. There was a lot less noise and no humans. What could be better? One highly intelligent and curious moose named Mashuga Moose noticed the strange quiet when it started. Mashuga Moose had been first at many things during his short moose life, but this first had him freaked out. If he couldn't hear the humans, how could he stay safe?"

People sounds warned moose and other forest wildlife when humans were close by; sometimes the animals would hide and other times they would just turn in the opposite direction, keeping their distance from the crazy humans. This was how forest wildlife, including Mashuga Moose, had stayed safe and away from people; Mashuga Moose was absolutely perplexed at the absence of the irritating people noises.

Mashuga Moose was reputed to be a highly professional and overachieving moose. "This moose was born to lead," had become the sentiment echoed by moose far and wide. The young moose, thinking only of the health and safety of all forest wildlife, made the choice to investigate "the strange quiet."

The Pandemic was scary and stressful for all of earths humans and animal wildlife. I created this book with the hope that it might help children experiencing pandemic related PTSD. Mashuga Moose is a humorous endearing moose who loves to provide a reason for a young moose or even a young human to smile and laugh. Just try saying "Mashuga Moose" ten-times, fast, I guarantee laughter.

IN THE TIME OF THE DENTED-PAN & THE STRANGE QUIET

"Waking-up in the time of the strange quiet."

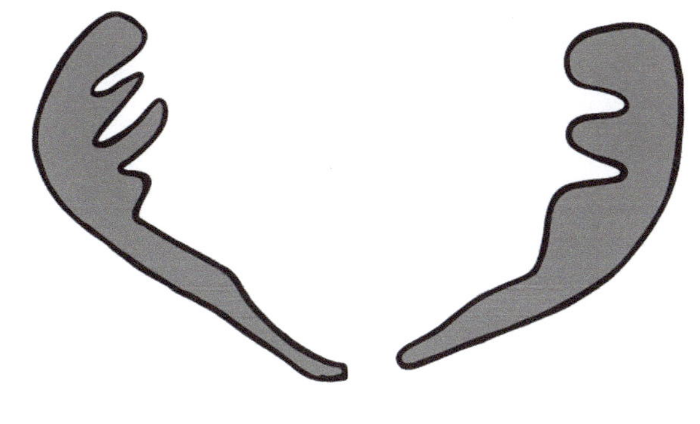

CHAPTER 1

A MOON SETS, AND A SUN COMES UP

The moon set over the western shore of Long Lake just as a young moose woke from a night of slumber.

During breakfast Mashuga Moose noticed that this morning's sunrise sounded different; something was not right.

Mashuga Moose listened in all directions; where were the people sounds? Why was it so quiet? What did this mean?

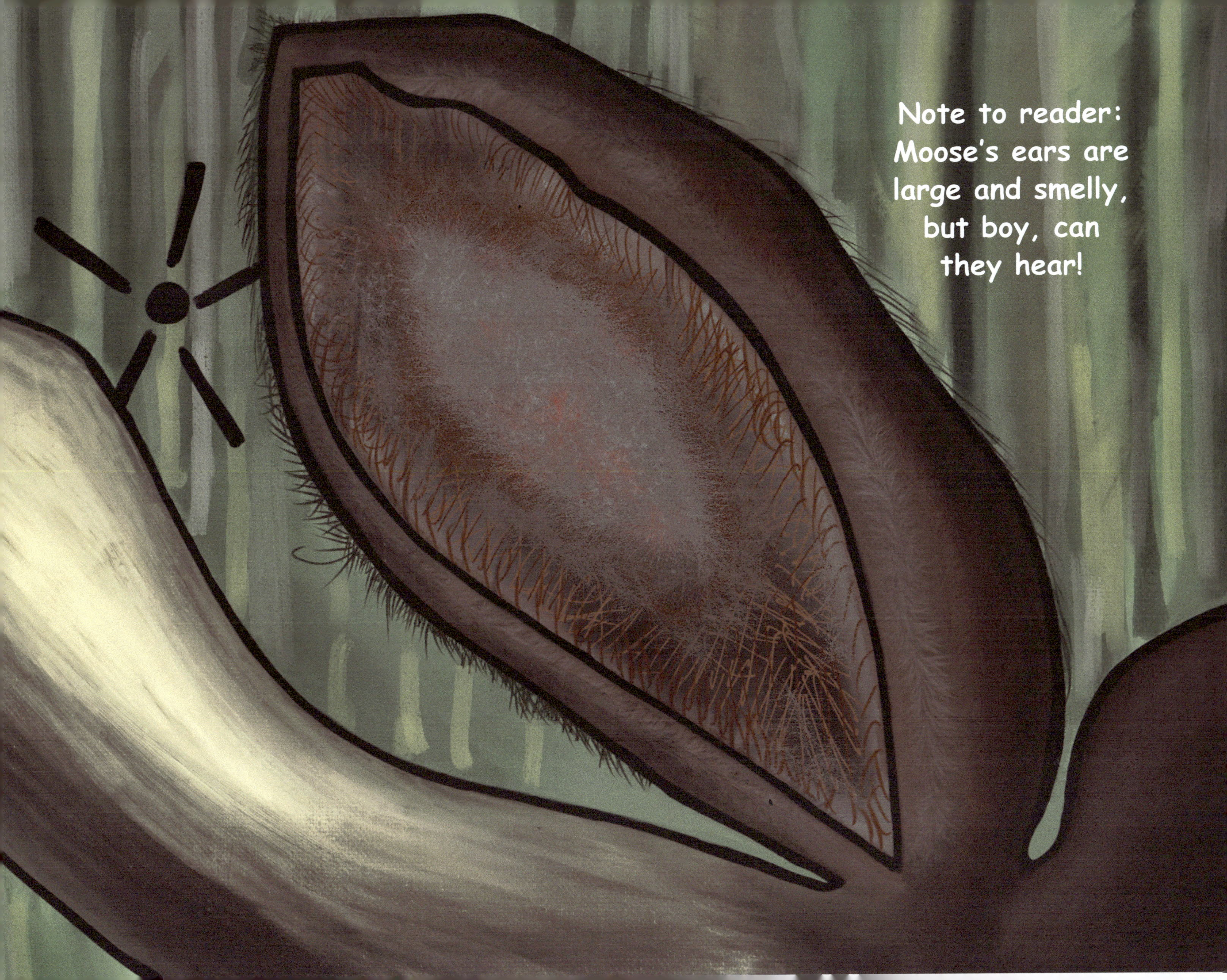

Note to reader:
Moose's ears are
large and smelly,
but boy, can
they hear!

The quiet was so disturbing it caused Mashuga Moose to wander into an area covered in very deep snow. On a positive note, while digging out of the deep snow he happened upon a nice selection of fresh willow bark. Once his stomach was full of willow bark, Mashuga Moose began his investigation.

No matter how hard he listened, "The Strange Quiet" was all he could hear, and that quiet had already spread to all the forest that he could hear. "I have to get closer to the village," Mashuga Moose thought.

CHAPTER 2

TOO QUIET FOR A MOOSE

The closer Mashuga Moose got to town, the more the quiet seemed to increase. "Why was this happening; what did it mean?" He had so many questions that needed just as many answers; he had to find the answers.

Mashuga Moose's Home
TOWN
SUGAR HOUSE SUNDAY
MAINE
MAPLE SYRUP

Mashuga Moose purposely took the path to town that went by the "Lake Ice," skating rink. There were no humans there either.

At the "Bus Barn" all the buses were locked and parked;
buses only make sounds if they are turned on.

It was quiet inside the bus.

Lake Region Bus Barn

CLOSED Due to COVID-19

Drivers Wanted

Good driver, eehhh.
Good with kids, yes!
$100 Signing Bonus.
On time to work.
Apply online now.

CHAPTER 3
MARTY'S FAMOUS SALT LICK

On his way to town, he stopped at Marty's famous salt lick.
When he arrived, no one was there.

Mashuga Moose consults with a very dear friend,

Moments later four of Mashuga Moose's moose
buddies arrived for a lick of salt.

When asked about the strange quiet, the other
moose just stared blankly straight ahead while continuing
to lick the salt off the side of the highway.

CHAPTER 4
MOOSE RIVER RESCUE

At the exact moment Mashuga Moose stepped onto the highway to continue his trip to the village, noise, lights, and speeding objects surrounded Mashuga Moose.

MOOSE RIVER
RESCUE

In shock from having a moose jump in front of his speeding ambulance, the driver caught a glimpse of the very lucky moose in his side-view mirror.

MOOSE RIVER
RESCUE

Mashuga Moose's friends were happy that he was OK.

His knees still weak and shaky, the young moose continued into town.

HEAVY
LOADS
LIMITED

Everywhere he went there was a strange silence.

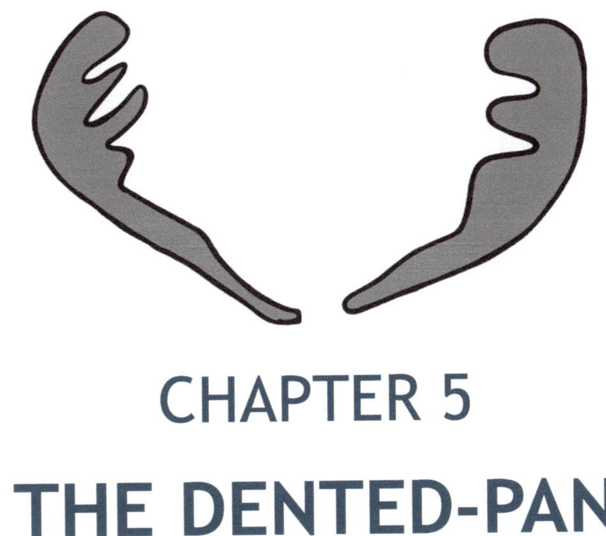

CHAPTER 5

THE DENTED-PAN

The strange quiet made Mashuga Moose feel worried and alone.

ETS
1SG

He hid behind a wall to stay safe.

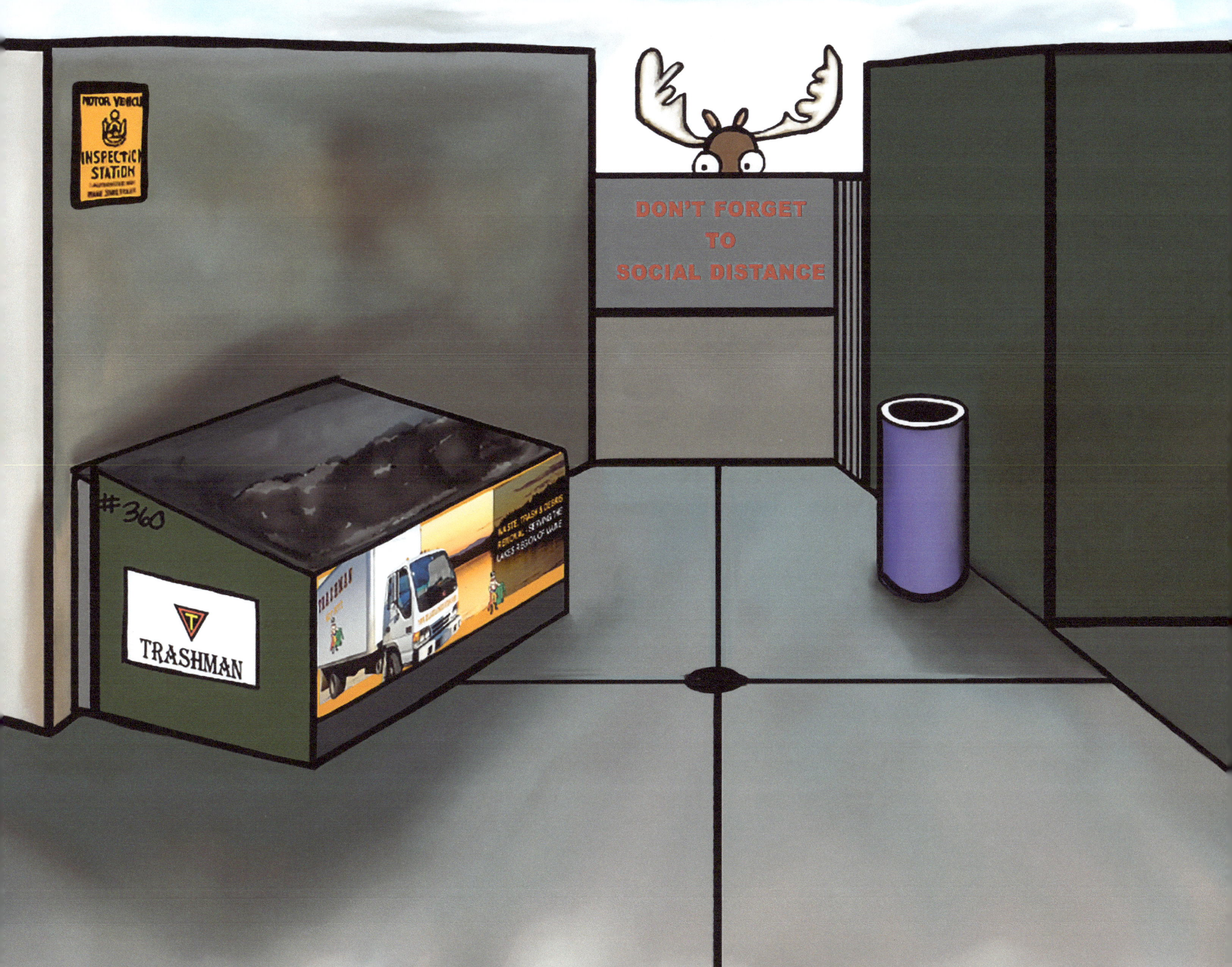
MOTOR VEHICLE
INSPECTION STATION
DON'T FORGET
TO
SOCIAL DISTANCE
#360
TRASHMAN
WASTE, TRASH & DEBRIS
REMOVAL   SERVING THE
LAKES REGION OF MAINE

The people inside the homes were quiet
when he looked in the house windows.

WE PAY $ FOR
TOILET PAPER.
To Trade: Fifty Pound of Black Beans
Wear Your Mask.
!Will barter for TP!
Need
Diapers - medium
Seasoned firewood 2 Cords

He felt better when he was in the shadows.

57

The "Moose Mercantile" sign read that
"everything was closed because of a "Dented-Pan."

SHIRLEY MY LOVE BIRD, THAT'S MASHUGA MOOSE
THAT'S ONE HANDSOME MOOSE.
+DENTED
SHUGA
OOSE
CAFE
Hours
CLOSED
EHAD
LE
OS
MOOSE
MERCANTILE
MOOSE RIVER, ME
25%
all Ice
Fishing
Supplies
CLOSED
DUE TO
PAN-
DEMIC
OFFICIAL
UNITED
STATES
POST
OFFICE
04055
HOURS:
CLOSED
Winter
Coats
Boots
Gloves
Long
Underwear

Just then another "wailing, flashing truck" passed. Mashuga Moose decided to follow the very noisy Red Truck.

INN
OPEN
FALLING ICE CAUTION
Falling ICE
GARDEN CENTER
ENTER
PARKING OFF STREET
CLOSED

CHAPTER 6

MEETING FRIENDS

The loud flashing Red Truck headed up the hill to a hospital for people.

MRH
Maine Regional Hospital

While climbing the hill he came upon his friends
"Larry Moose and Mad Marge Moose."

Mad Marge Moose suggested Mashuga Moose check out the woods
behind her. Mashuga Moose walked down a short path and exited the
forest into a world of people noises and lights.

CHAPTER 7

NOT A PLACE FOR A MOOSE

The young moose wanted to be back in his forest where he was safe
and it was quiet. He wanted to run away, but his curiosity kept his feet
planted firmly in the spring snow.

He had been searching for noise all day,
now all he wanted was quiet, and some willow bark.

COVID-19 TESTING?
HOSPITAL EMERGENCIES
NAPLES RESCUE
JACKMAN RESCUE

It was curiosity that had kept Mashuga Moose from running away; it also caused him to keep getting closer to the glass windows of the hospital. Somehow Mashuga Moose found himself standing in front of the emergency department entrance doors.

COVID-19 ONLY!
EMERGENCY
ENTRANCE
Testing, check at Red Cross Tents.

No sooner had the people in the hospital noticed the moose at the door, than the panicked moose was running away. When a moose is afraid there is only one word that can fit in their brain, that word is "RUN." So, he ran!

RUN

He ran across a road without looking both ways.

He ran so fast that the word that filled his brain looked backwards,
so he ran even faster.

Mashuga Moose's friends watched from the forest's edge as he plunged into a stream filled with very cold melted winter snow water. Moments later he was on the other shoreline running even faster.

Mashuga Moose had searched all day for the sounds that a
moose would listen for to stay safe in the forest.

Yet, each time he found those sounds,
all he wanted to do was to run away.

RUN

CHAPTER 8

HE'S NOT ALONE

He ran through a stand of birch trees without changing direction or speed.
A mile later he stopped. Steamy sweat rose from the moose's coat.

The moose's brain had become filled with the image
of a Stop Sign, so he stopped.

STOP

The lights in the sky above his head were causing Mashuga Moose to begin to panic. The gigantic moose was again thinking of running away. At that exact same moment two moose voices emanated from behind Mashuga Moose: "Larry Moose and Mad Marge Moose had followed Mashuga Moose all the way from the hospital. With the added company of the other moose, Mashuga Moose's anxiety seemed to disappear.

He was so happy to see his best moose buddies, yet Mashuga Moose
still had a very important question to ask his friends.
Mashuga Moose turned to his two friends and asked calmly,
"Is the sky falling; are we about to become extinct?"

Mad Marge Moose said, "The sky is not falling,
And Larry Moose and I are here for you."

Larry Moose said, "Hey brother moose, the lights in the sky are the
'Aurora Borealis,' Mashuga Moose's brain filled with the word, "WHAT?"

On that night the Aurora Borealis was visible
throughout the northern forest.

The three moose watched as the solar winds collided
with the earths ionosphere and glowed in the sky above.

Larry Moose, Mad Marge Moose and Mashuga Moose
stood side by side looking up at the sky.

For that moment the "Strange Quiet" and the "Dented-Pan" were
replaced by the natural wonder occurring in the heavens above.

No matter man or moose, the Northern Lights were magical to see.

Mashuga Moose wondered if the "Dented Pan and the
"Strange quiet, and this Borealis thing were connected.

The young Moose was sure of one thing,
the Aurora Borealis was beautiful.

Why a Dented-Pan? It's simple, Mashuga Moose was reading-challenged. When he read the sign that was on "The Moose Mercantile" window, that read "CLOSED DUE TO PANDEMIC, in his mind he heard, "Due to a Dented-Pan." The wildlife embraced the name, crediting Mashuga Moose with solving the mystery.

AND
THE
STRANGE
QUIET
IN THE TIME
OF THE
DENTED-PAN

And the Strange Quiet?

In an attempt to slow the spread of the covid virus, so that medical systems around the world would not be overwhelmed, people around the world who could, self-isolated at home.

The planes stopped flying, the trains stopped running, and most ships around the world dropped their anchors where they floated, waiting till the day the "Strange Quiet" ended.

The once noisy human work environments were now surprisingly quiet. This was when, around the world, the forest wildlife began to venture into the cities, towns and villages.

The wildlife moved into the areas where people normally played and worked. While the little animals of the forest never fully understood what had happened, they appreciated the fine shrubbery and annuals the people had made available for their consumption.

EPILOGUE/CONCLUSION

Additional information regarding Mashuga Moose.

1) Mashuga Moose was dyslexic and was non-normative "ADHD" as related to his placement on the "Moose Behavioral Spectrum." The challenges of dealing with a learning and behavioral deficit was a serious challenge for a young moose. Mashuga Moose learned to understand his behaviors, as well as their impact.

2) Mashuga Moose can read. This was a great surprise because Moose have very poor eyesight, and they usually do not attend school. They are also not able to carry a book bag. Experts were constantly being surprised by Mashuga Moose and his ever-expanding vocabulary.

Join Mashuga Moose and the other Moose
in their next north woods adventure.

ABOUT THE AUTHOR

Allan Rosen-Ducat grew up in Philadelphia's western suburbs. He became an amateur photographer at age twelve, an interest that never waned.

Rosen-Ducat was diagnosed dyslexic in second grade and diagnosed ADHD at age fifty. Allan studied art at Ohio Wesleyan University in Delaware, Ohio, transferring to

Rochester Institute of Technology, where he graduated with a BFA in Photographic Illustration. Moving to Southern California in his twenties, Maine in his thirties, and then back to the Southwest's Phoenix, Arizona, when he was in his forties.

When asked about the book effort Rosen-Ducat stated the following.

"Mashuga Moose's adventure begins on the day that many of the nations of the world took steps to limit the spread of the novel "COVID-19 virus." Fearing the collapse of hospital networks government leaders initiated an 'at home' isolation policy, the effort was one of global reach; billions of workers stayed home, schools closed and we watched a pandemic explode on a highspeed network stream.

The start of the Pandemic was scary for children and their parents; no one knew what humanity was looking at. Would the "COVID-19 virus" decimate the world's human population as did the *magna mortalitas*," as it was known in the Middle Ages as the, "Great Mortality," which today is commonly known as "The Black Death." No one knew what would happen.

The global spread of the novel virus created new rules to follow. Most humans did their best adapting to staying at home, this was hardest for people who lived alone and or needed assistance. As the adaptations became the new normal, in the cities the sound of ambulance sirens seemed to be present all day and all night.

Humans had to adjust to the change, but how would they know what was safe and what was not.

Mashuga Moose had the same issue. Humans make so much noise that wildlife has an easy time keeping track of us while we are visiting the forest. The change caused to the soundscape surrounding the forest where Mashuga Moose lived was so impactful, that some of the animals began experiencing bouts of anxiety. This is why Mashuga Moose attempted to solve the mystery. He needed human noises to be safe.